Neelanjana is currently a student. She is passionate about writing, having written short stories or fan fictions for a while. She believes poems are a medium to express her innermost emotions, she enjoys filling her pages with marvelous verses. She is a big music fanatic, who listens to all sorts of genres. Being a dreamer, she was forced at several points to give up, but her heart is too stubborn. Beaches and ocean water calms her busy mind.

Nubepollis

Neelanjana Anne

AUSTIN MACAULEY PUBLISHERS
LONDON • CAMBRIDGE • NEW YORK • SHARJAH

Copyright © **Neelanjana Anne** 2023

The right of **Neelanjana Anne** to be identified as author of this work has been asserted by by the author in accordance with Federal Law No. (7) of UAE, Year 2002, Concerning Copyrights and Neighboring Rights.

All rights reserved. No part of this publication may be reproduced, stored in a retrieval system, or transmitted in any form or by any means, electronic, mechanical, photocopying, recording, or otherwise, without the prior permission of the publishers.

Any person who commits any unauthorized act in relation to this publication may be liable to legal prosecution and civil claims for damages.

This is a work of fiction. Names, characters, businesses, places, events, locales, and incidents are either the products of the author's imagination or used in a fictitious manner. Any resemblance to actual persons, living or dead, or actual events is purely coincidental.

The age group that matches the content of the books has been classified according to the age classification system issued by the Ministry of Culture and Youth.

ISBN – 9789948802471 – (Paperback)
ISBN – 9789948802488 – (E-Book)

Application Number: MC-10-01-9672417
Age Classification: E

First Published 2023
AUSTIN MACAULEY PUBLISHERS FZE
Sharjah Publishing City
P.O. Box [519201]
Sharjah, UAE
www.austinmacauley.ae
+971 655 95 202

This book is dedicated to all the dreamers. Let your spirit remain unshattered.

I would like to first express my gratitude to my father for supporting me during the rough ride I had while writing the book and my mother for pushing me forward when I couldn't write.

Thank you, Austin Macauley Publishers, for resolving my doubts and overseeing the book's production. I would also like to thank the illustrations department for bringing the characters to life with their images and the editorial team for their marvellous work in rectifying the text.

Finally, I would like to acknowledge everyone who has touched my life with their words of wisdom and companionship.

The Christmas Star

"Josh, it's getting dark and dinner's ready." I heard Pappy call me home. "Pappy, two minutes, I'm watching these beetles fight." They were fighting, trying to push the other one away, Pappy told me it was to impress the female beetle. Pappy stepped out into the front porch and placed his hands on his hips, he glared into my soul.

"Joshua, you better come inside, I'm not going to repeat myself." This meant trouble, he only called me Joshua when he was angry or annoyed with me.

"Yes Sir!" I say and run back into the house.
I live with my grandpa, everyone calls him Billy or Mr. Johnson, I call him Pappy, it's grandpa with respect and love. My mother passed away when I was quite young and grandma doesn't live with us anymore.
Papa works away from home, we visit him every summer, sometimes he comes home for Thanksgiving or Christmas or Easter and other holidays. I miss Papa a lot. He once bought a telescope for my birthday.

"Wash your face and hands properly," Pappy ordered. He set the dishes out on the table; I sniffed the air only to smell the goodness of food. My stomach grumbled, Pappy heard it and started chuckling, "Son, sit down and say grace." We held hands and said grace. Pappy learned to cook a while after grandma left, that was a few years ago, now I'm proud to say that I'm ten.

"Pass me the beans." he asked, I served him. I inhaled into my food, gobbled it up. "Slow down, you will get sick if you eat that fast." I slowed my pace and completed it. Well, no matter how fast I eat, Pappy's always first, he eats a lot more than me. I guess when you grow

older you can learn to eat more and fast. We had a telly in the house but Pappy restricted me from using it, he promised to buy one for my 12th birthday. He said it's because he doesn't want me to spend my time in front of the TV. We did have a fabulous radio though; the voices were heard crystal clear. On Saturdays and Sundays, it was game night and we supported the red sock. "And...that's a home run" they would announce only for us to jump about in excitement. Today a different voice came out of the box. I recognized that old, raspy voice immediately. It was Tom Fittleton, the old astronomer. He broadcasted every Monday, Wednesday, and Friday. It was

surprising to hear his broadcast today, after all, it was Thursday.
I glanced at Pappy looking confused, he said "It must be a special broadcast, the stars never align on fixed dates."
I nodded my head and agreed, yes, sometimes I can make sense of what adults speak, I'm a grown-up.
"You folks must be wondering about this special broadcast. It is indeed special..." he sounded joyful today. I was on my feet and getting fired up, gazing at the night sky has always been my favorite thing.

Pappy and I would sometimes camp outside, just to gaze at those small bright dots, those stars mesmerized us. Pappy always said that I reminded him of papa, apparently, he too loved the starry sky and went to work for NASA. Pappy was proud of his son, and I too was proud of my dad. He was one of the very few people in mission control the day we launched a man into the moon.

Pappy had a telly in his room, and it was only used for such special occasions. I keep reminding him, the promise he made for my 12th birthday.

"So, folks, I suggest you bring out your navigating map of the sky today and note down the coordinates as well as the timings."

He didn't have to mention more, I already had it all ready the minute he started broadcasting. Pappy ruffled my hair and set the map on the table in our hall.

"You must observe this Christmas star, it is not a star, but the great Jupiter and Saturn will be so close, that the brightness makes it appear like an actual star.

Folks, you don't wanna miss this, it's super rare, such a cosmological event will not happen for the next 800 years!

The entire scientific community is geared up to witness this celestial magic, and you must too..." he trailed away.

I was hopping with excitement and Pappy tried to calm me down.

"Sshh... Let me hear what he's saying, Josh!" Pappy said with clear annoyance on his face. "So, folks, I'm back with the timings for your region when you can watch this spectacular event.

Scopes located in the Eastern United States will be able to catch Ganymede as it transits Jupiter for three and a half hours starting at 7:04 p.m. EST. Meanwhile, telescopic observers on the West coast will see Ganymede's shadow hovering over Jupiter's cloud tops by 9:40 p.m. EST."

Pappy noted down some details, I couldn't understand what Mr. Fittleton was blabbering over the radio. He didn't stop talking for the next half an hour, and Pappy's ears were glued to the radio likewise.

I know that I will understand it by the time I'm 12, looks like all the good things will happen to me when I'm 12.

But, I'm better off than my buddies, Ethan and Nate. They don't know the ABCs of astronomy, in fact, I'm the only 10-year-old in the entire of Luckenbach who can point out major constellations in the night sky.

Some people may think that I'm a geek, but they don't know how much fun I and my buddies have. We watch the telly for hours in Nate's house. So many shows, I like Wonder Woman, my buddies swore that they would never tell this to anyone, especially Pappy. I shudder at the thought itself; he'll flay my skin out.

"Go to bed junior, it's quite late already," Pappy said, getting up from the chair.
He made me brush my teeth, change into my pajamas, and tucked me in. Pappy liked discipline a lot, he made sure I was a well-behaved lad.
"Pappy, are we going to see the Christmas star?" I asked to hope for a yes.
"Josh, if you promise to complete your homework and do the chores tomorrow without my help, then we can navigate the Christmas star." Pappy was good at negotiating and I knew that deep inside he already agreed to this without my asking.
I smiled and whispered 'yes'.

He leaned in and gave me a goodnight kiss, "Good night junior, tomorrow's a long day for you."
He leaves the lamplight on, I get terrified in the dark, once I heard the floor creak and since then I have started believing that there's a monster under my bed.
Pappy doesn't believe me, he says that it's all in my head and if I'm a brave boy, then I can defeat this creepy monster.
Pappy is a good storyteller, he used to write books and was a really famous author. I wonder what kind of stories he wrote. I still struggle to read those big, fat books.
My eyes started feeling heavy and I yawned into the silence.

The Creek

The school bell rang loud enough for all of us to pack our stuff. Miss Mason sighed, she always seems to do this, I guess she dislikes having to teach us at the last period.

Before Miss Mason asked us to leave, I was already on my way. "Where do you think you're going, young man?" she asked sternly. Her eyebrows now narrowed and her face looked serious. "Miss, I'm going home," I replied, turning ahead again.

She caught the hem of my shirt and pulled me back. "Now, listen to me Josh,

you are going nowhere with that wild behavior of yours." I realized that she hadn't dismissed us yet. I was so caught up with the stargazing event today, that nothing mattered more to me. Pappy would be disappointed if he'd learn about this reckless action of mine, so before things could go out of control I apologized.

"I'm terribly sorry, Miss Mason, I presumed you already asked us to leave. You see Ma'am, I am quite excited because I'm doing something special this evening."

Her face twisted and she raised her eyebrows.

The entire class started roaring with laughter, I gave my most appealing smile. "Young boy, I'm leaving you today but remember you are not to repeat this again." She said with a look of distaste. "Yes, Ma'am," I pronounced loud and clear. "Class dismissed!" She announced and I ran into the corridor packed with kids. "I should've never signed up to teach fifth graders, they're a handful," Miss Mason muttered under her breath.
I dashed out into the sunny road and skipped a few steps to stop right in front of my bus. The yellow giant humbled all the other cars around.

"Hey Josh, why're you so happy, man?" Big Ben asked me. Big Ben was one of the finest bus drivers you'd ever find. I'd hire him if I owned a bus. Most bus rides get bumpy near the speed breakers, but Big Ben would sail this thing as if the bump never existed.
He always had a coffee mug near the dashboard, he had a small black mustache. Pappy had a mustache too and his face was wrinkled.
Big Ben is a generous man too, rare ones they say.
He would wait for a few minutes if I ever got late, he honks twice and that's the cue for my ride.

I grinned and replied, "Today I'm gonna see a Christmas star Big Ben, and it's a super rare sight."
"A Christmas star, it's not even Christmas yet!" he comments. "Well anyways, I haven't seen Nate with you?" he asked with concern.
Nate didn't come to school today. Yesterday after we came back from a hike to the other neighborhood, Nate said that he wasn't feeling well.
We all stopped our bikes, Nate flung out from his bike, that red thing hit the ground with a thud.
Nate puked out on the pavement. I was disgusted at the sight that held before.

Floods of pale vomit and a horrid stench along with it. Ugh!
We took him home, luckily his house was only a few blocks away. That boy held onto me, while Ethan dragged our bikes with great difficulty.
After that incident, Ethan called me up saying that he wasn't feeling well. I guess some grub must have caused it. Germs are too dangerous.
"He and Ethan fell sick, I guess some stomach grub did it all," I replied.
"Well, you stay safe, I've heard them saying it's flu season out here, now go get yourself seated." he motioned me to one of the seats.

I sat down and kept thinking of my buddies throughout the bus ride.
"Pappy, I'm home!" I say kicking my boots off.
"Pappy..." I went searching for that old man. He was talking with someone over the phone.
"I see Mrs. Hudson." I tugged his free hand and signaled him asking who it was.
"Mrs. Hudson, I do hope Ethan recovers, yes, we will be praying for him to get better soon. Thank you, Mrs. Hudson, have a great day." He cut the line.
"How are they? Did it get serious? Are they gonna get a few injections?" Curiosity getting the better of me.

"Nothing Josh, they're just taking rest, and no, don't anticipate any injections." I sighed with relief.

"Junior, I wonder how you didn't end up sick. Probably you have good immunity."

I nodded my head.

"Now come along and freshen up, I will heat the dinner, we should set our camp near the creek," Pappy explained.

I jumped up saying 'Hurray'.

I planned on getting ready soon since it would give me extra time to sneak in some Marshmallows. We packed our stuff and had our dinner. Pappy bought the big tent along with many other pieces of equipment.

Pappy opened the garage gate, only to reveal his gorgeous truck. Chevy El Camino, Pappy's pride and beauty. Pappy poured his heart and soul into maintaining this truck, it was a 1965 model. He calls it 'Chevy'. Every time he looks at his possession, a smile automatically gets plastered on his face. It was a Danube Blue; I won't forget the color.

When we ride this big girl out in the neighborhood, I feel rich. The shade of blue is so pompous, such a shade that inspires one to accomplish things. It is deep blue, inclined to indigo.

"Mr. Bassett's gonna turn red as a

beetroot," Pappy remarked, bringing me to the ground.

We had an adventure awaiting us and I couldn't let myself get distracted with thoughts of such beauty.

This would generally happen but not today.

Pappy would already get himself seated, and I would join him in the front. He always manages to catch me red-handed. "Joshua, rules are rules, kids are not allowed to sit in the front." He would order and I sulk in the backseat.

Today, I grinned at Pappy, he knew why and accepted his defeat. "You have to put your seatbelt on young man, else I'm

leaving you behind." he warned, looking straight in my eye.

"Yes, Sir!" I saluted and fastened my seat belt.

Pappy had this sort of tradition, every time he passes Mister Bassett, he honks to let his presence be known.

They both have a clash I imply; they don't see eye to eye but Pappy always ends up playing cards and having fried chicken from the Bassetts.

I simply smile outside and wave to Jessica Bassett. She has an angelic smile, I like her a lot, but too bad she's an eighth-grader. She is really friendly

and kind.
We passed the sunsetting streets, with youngsters still roaming around, boys playing baseball. There was no traffic, we never found much in our streets, but out on the main road, it's nothing
but hell.
Pappy turned the radio on and started humming. He seemed to be in high spirits, we both always do when we're out. Fly Me to the moon, our favorite was blasting loudly on the speaker. "Sonny, Music is beautiful, I wish you played piano. Your mother wanted to

see you playing it, she loved art." Pappy chatted reminiscently.

I've never heard this before; Pappy rarely talks about my mother. I don't feel miserable or sad because I don't remember how she was.

I've missed how it feels like to have lunch prepared by soft hands, the same hand which would wave at me as I boarded the yellow bus.

Pappy showed affection but it was more manly. He would ruffle my hair, sometimes peck my cheek and pat my back.

"Pappy, tell me more," I asked with sparkling eyes.

"She was a strong woman, she did a few plays," he replied, steering the car.
"Play?"
"Yes, your mother was an actress. She lived her role, she got cast on Broadway once, oh! How your father with great difficulty obtained a seat in the front row, only to see his darling perform. In the end, he would stand up, applaud and whistle for the outstanding performance. They never let her rise to the top, they didn't let that charm shine, crooked people and horrid times. She couldn't bear it, those petty small-time roles she had to play.
With you in her womb, she left it all and

settled down," he narrated.
Pappy and I did share a big enthusiasm for movie night, he would play old classics, new comedies, and award-winning movies.
He stopped the Chevy on the metalled road. I got down, unfastening my seat belt. Pappy parked the car near the curb. We were two miles away from the town, near the creek where it's the best for stargazing. We didn't have to worry about wild animals apart from raccoons and possums.
I held two bags and he carried the heavy stuff.
The radio was the most important thing along with our prized telescope.

As we walked into the woods, our feet crunched the floor. It was dark, but we were able to make out the path thanks to the moonlight and the torch.
I could hear the stream flowing, and ran ahead. Nothing to be afraid of since the woods aren't as deep as you think and I had Pappy. I'm certain he could take on any mobsters.
I inhaled the fresh air, it smelt of musk. Pebbled shore guarded the stream, which danced down the trail. It was a slow stream, speeded only on rainy days. It was crystal clear as I could see my own reflection in
the moonlight.
Pappy started unpacking and brought

out the tent. It wasn't a fancy one, quite simple instead. It was pale cream in color and two people could fit in. We would stay warm and zipped in during the night, it also prevents any bugs or critters from entering.

I slipped off my shoes and advanced to the stream. It was slow and calm, I couldn't resist anymore. I dipped my feet slowly into the flowing water.

To my surprise it was mildly warm after all, anyone would expect the water to be freezing cold. "Pappy!" I cried with joy. He looked tense for a second and asked me if anything was wrong. "The water is

warm and not cold" I started chuckling, Pappy gave a grin and continued.

We settled down after a while, I had to collect some wood sticks.

Pappy set up the camp and the telescope.

We were tuned in for any information on the radio.

I did the waiting, Pappy in the meantime would use his astronomical instruments and find our star.

"Josh, come here quick!" Pappy called out for me.

"It's beautiful, dear god, blessed we are, truly," he mumbled while I peered into the scope.

My eyes adjusted themselves and
I saw the magic.
It glowed like a thousand suns; the luminosity was so calm. It was bright, it lit up everything around it.
A beauty so celestial and heavenly, it was just like another Christmas star,
but even better.
Pappy and I took turns, we even made out a few constellations and other elements in the night sky.
He called it the marvelous gift of nature.

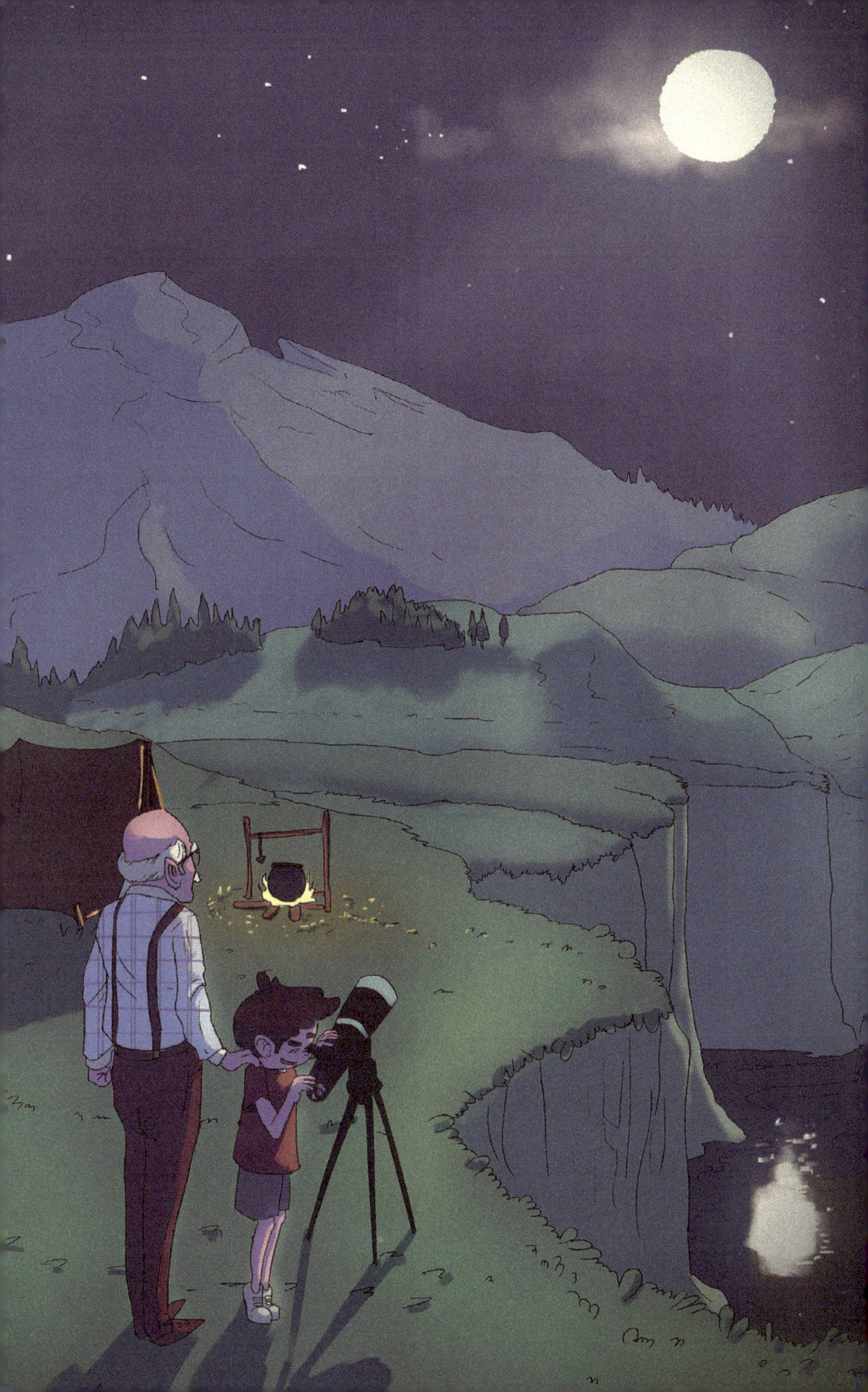

We then roasted some marshmallows that I sneaked in, he did warn me not to repeat it, but since they were tasting good, he didn't nag me much.

"Son, remember the stars are our ancestors, they look upon us and take care of us from above. All the dead go to heaven and God transforms them into stars so that they can keep shining brightly to give hope and provide light for all of us on earth," Pappy explained.

There was a moment of silence while I tried to digest what I was told. "Pappy, is Mama up there too?"

"Josh, she is up there, she misses us but is happy to share her light."

"Now let's go and sleep. It's getting late junior," he ordered.

"Yes sir." I hopped into our tent. After we settled in, I snuggled close to Pappy and whispered, "Pappy, I'm not able to fall asleep"

He doesn't budge. "Pappy... Pappy..." I hissed.

"What is it, Joshua?" he asks, shifting around.

"I'm not sleepy and I'm scared," I say meekly.

"Do you want me to tell a story?" he asks.

I hum a yes. "Remember don't interrupt me in between for no reason," he warned.

"Roger," I replied.

The Pilot Who Touched the Clouds

"Josh, do you know that there's a whole world out there?" Pappy asked me, while I snuggled close to him.
"The stars?" I asked uncertainly.
Pappy smiled and replied "Looks like you don't know about it. Let me tell you."
The clouds we see above aren't just clouds, they are more than that. The clouds are home to many creatures. Have you ever wondered why you were able to make out the shapes that clouds take? Sometimes you can point out a cloud on a bright sunny day and say that it looks like a dog!

Let me tell you a secret, in fact, it is not known to many.
You should consider yourself lucky to hear what I'm narrating now.
The white clouds you see in the pastel blue sky are copycats! They see different animals, birds, humans, trees, items, and many others which are present on the land, in our cities, towns, and households only to amuse themselves by impersonating us.
They find it really fun to imitate our things and animals.
You mustn't be surprised if they hold

competitions for imitation.
So, the next time you gaze at these fluffy clouds don't forget they like to mimic us, they mimic your face.
Now, I'm reminded of something that may seem trivial to you.
The Chukaku trees...
Go ahead laugh all you can, this wasn't named by us, the cloud nymphs were responsible for it.
The best part of those tall, faded green trees is the fruit. Commonly called the 'Chika' fruit.
Again, you're giggling. I too guffawed at these names when my father passed down this knowledge.

Yes, my father was an explorer, I respected him a lot for that. I wasn't cut out for exploring and traveling the world, but I am excellent at bringing the world to my desk.
The books I write son, they're all stories which allow my readers to travel and live in different worlds just at their place."
I only listened to the recount with great amazement. Pappy continued.
"Now, where was I... Yes, the pilot. Oh, indeed that is the power of the Chika fruit.
There was a pilot who loved to soar around in the big sky, he could be heard with his motor engine and the airplane.

He zoomed in and out, twirled, and performed marvelous loops, lunging at fluffy clouds.

He was one of a kind, the best pilot I ever heard of. Will you believe that he stepped out of his plane in midair just to catch a Chika fruit?

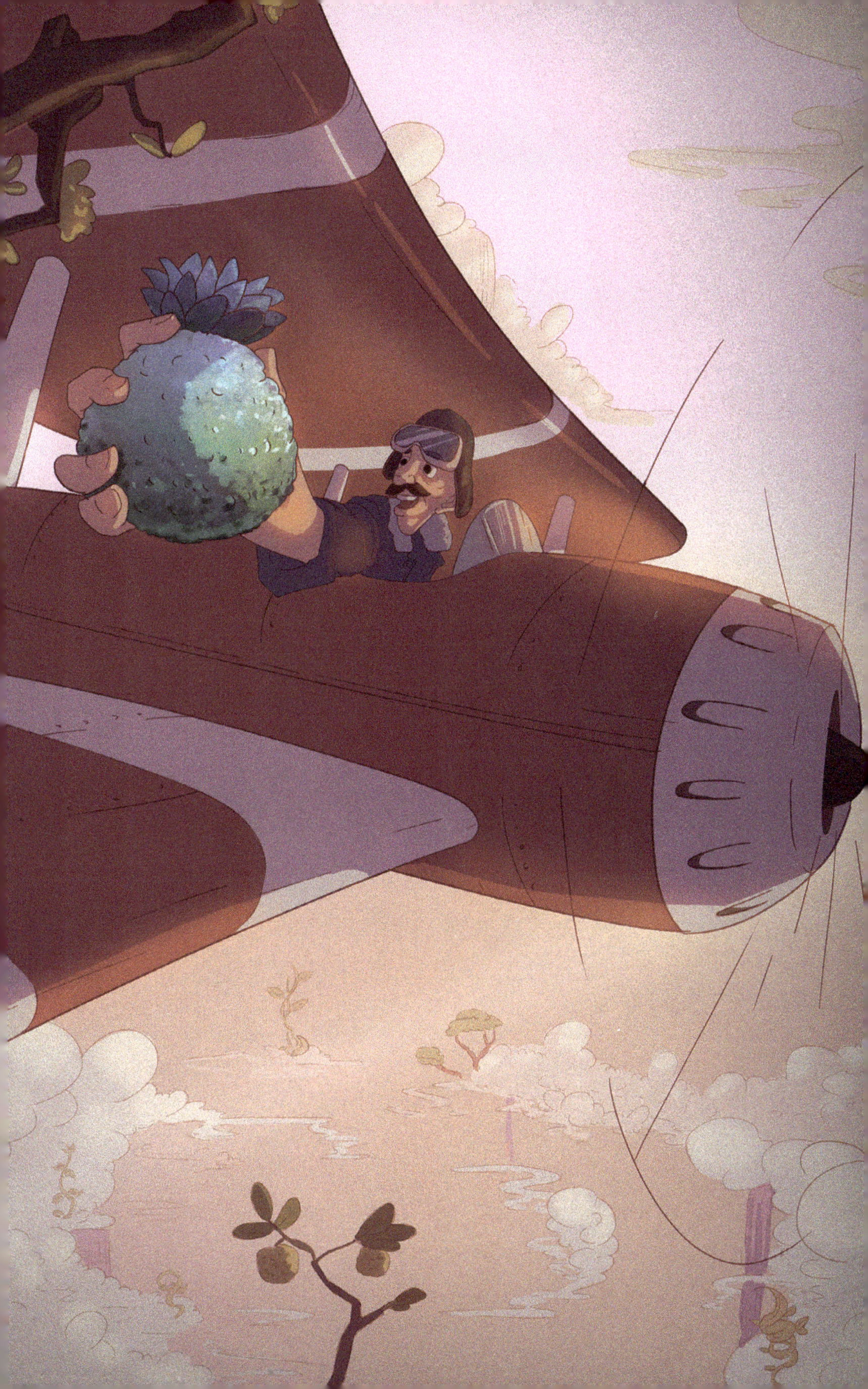

He didn't fall, every pilot has their own tricks up their sleeve.
He managed to land safely in the plainlands.
The Chika fruit held like an achievement in his hand. It had the shape of a peach, its soft skin, colored in different shades of blue, From dark indigo to arctic pale. It was prickly with thorns on the top, like a crown on its head. The pilot carefully cut it open with his pocketknife unable to resist the sweet scent it was giving away.

Blue juices spilled down as he grazed the fruit.

He inhaled the sweet fragrant and bit into its pale blue flesh.

"Chika! I want more of these Chikas... Chika..." he yammered.

I have to say there is a reason why they call it the forbidden fruit. Humans go crazy after tasting it just how our pilot did here.

He craved more and more for the fruit; he became inseparable from the Chika fruit.

There's an exception here, the nymphs and children can taste a Chika and resist all temptations. This is because children are said to have a pure heart. Uncorrupted souls and strong will.
The pilot brought over a hundred Chikas and tried planting their purple seeds in the soil. Foolish he became, for how can a Chika grow on land?
Chikas are rare since they can only be harvested in the cloud environment. The seed never grew, he waited for 6 months, then a year, and realized they were never gonna grow into trees.

He became furious and disappointed with his failure; he went again to the clouds now driven by the ambition to directly kidnap the Chukaku trees.

The pilot drained all of his luck; the authorities stopped him before he could endanger the Chukaku trees.

He was dragged to doctors who took care of him,

"My Chikas... They're mine! Don't you dare touch them! Chikas!" he yelled furiously before being driven away to a hospital.

"Pappy, who eats those Chika fruits?" I asked curiously.

"Well, the inhabitants of the clouds.
The creeper is a grub, which feeds on Chukaku leaves, the birds there white as snow feed on these creepers and Chikas.
I think these small birds are
called stockers.
Yes, yes, they're called stockers.
These are not the only animals who live in clouds, there are plenty of others.
The clouds always have water and this makes life flourish there.

Whenever they have excess water, it rains here on earth. These rains help our fields, farms, forests and much more to be replenished with freshwater."

I interrupted him and asked, "Do I have a pure heart?"

Pappy just smiled and ruffled my hair, "Yes, my boy you do. All children do have pure hearts. You are my angel, so don't worry about eating the Chika fruits when you see one."

I smiled and reminded him, "Pappy, please continue. I am still not sleepy"

Nubepollis

Pappy shifted a bit and settled down comfortably. "The cloud nymphs are wonderful beings. You can always tell one apart from us, they have very distinct features, easy to identify. I'll teach you it's quite simple...
The cloud nymphs are indeed magical and beautiful. They have otherworldly beauty.
Cloud nymphs are like humans, they walk on their legs and use their hands. Their faces are equally alike but on another level.

The skin is the first way to identify a cloud nymph, two colors:
Mustard Yellow or Baby Blue.
Do you know how the skin tone of a baby is decided?
If the baby is born during the day, they get a mustard yellow and if the baby is born at night, they turn blue.
Secondly, they have pointed ears, they're quite similar to us at the same time.
There are many cities in the cloud world, but the closest one to us is Nubepollis.

Ah, the grand architecture, golden buildings, cloud roads, and shimmering houses. Most of their homes and offices don't have any doors or completely closed walls.

They have a roof overhead and some pillars. Naturally, the Nymphs feel suffocated in closed rooms and prefer open spaces.

Now, this is the most interesting thing we know about the Nymphs. They sleep during the day and work during the night. Absurd... Isn't it? But the reason behind these weird timings is because they give us dreams."

"What are you saying, Pappy?!"

I was very startled.

"Now, don't jump the gun and go ahead of yourself, I'm here to explain. Every being on earth has a purpose and job.

For example, Josh, your job as a child is to listen to your elders, learn what is good, what is bad, and about our world. You must learn how this world works, why anything happens, you must stay curious as it will take you to incredible places, just how my father's thirst for knowledge led him to the discovery of Nubepollis and the remaining cloud world, you too will stumble upon, invent something that will serve us all.

Another example, your teacher, Ms.

Mason, whose duty is to educate children not only in their school studies but also on values and out-of-the-book knowledge. This is because the entire future of this country, or the world lies in the hands of the children. When these children grow up to be responsible and smart adults with manners and values, they can change the face of our nation. They can improve society and develop us furthermore.

Now, in the same manner, the Nymphs were given some amazing special powers. These powers enabled them to provide dreams to all the beings on earth.

There is a lot of suffering and misery

all around us, to retain hope, we dream. These dreams give us the willpower to achieve something, to live another day, they show us the unlimited potential we have in store.

The Nymphs during the night, when the entire world snores loudly, release their magic. This magic is harvested in the moonlight using stardust.

They slip into our minds and show us dreams which make us happy."

"Pappy then what about nightmares?" I interrupted.

"Oh Josh, would you just let me complete?!" Pappy replied.

"Nightmares happen only because a Nymph hasn't entered your mind or you didn't sleep properly making it difficult

for a Nymph to work their magic on you. The nymphs have their own offices and set of rules they must follow.
I have to say it's a great job they're doing out there. They're spreading hope for a better day, they're motivating the lost souls to find their homes.
Remember Josh, Always thank the Nymphs whenever you receive a good dream.
Now, I'm tired, thanks to all the talking and storytelling.
You better sleep, junior."
"Good night, Pappy and thank you," I said, giving him a warm hug.
"Thank you for what?" he asked.
"For revealing the secret of the cloud world." A smile plastered on his face. He kissed my forehead and put me to sleep.

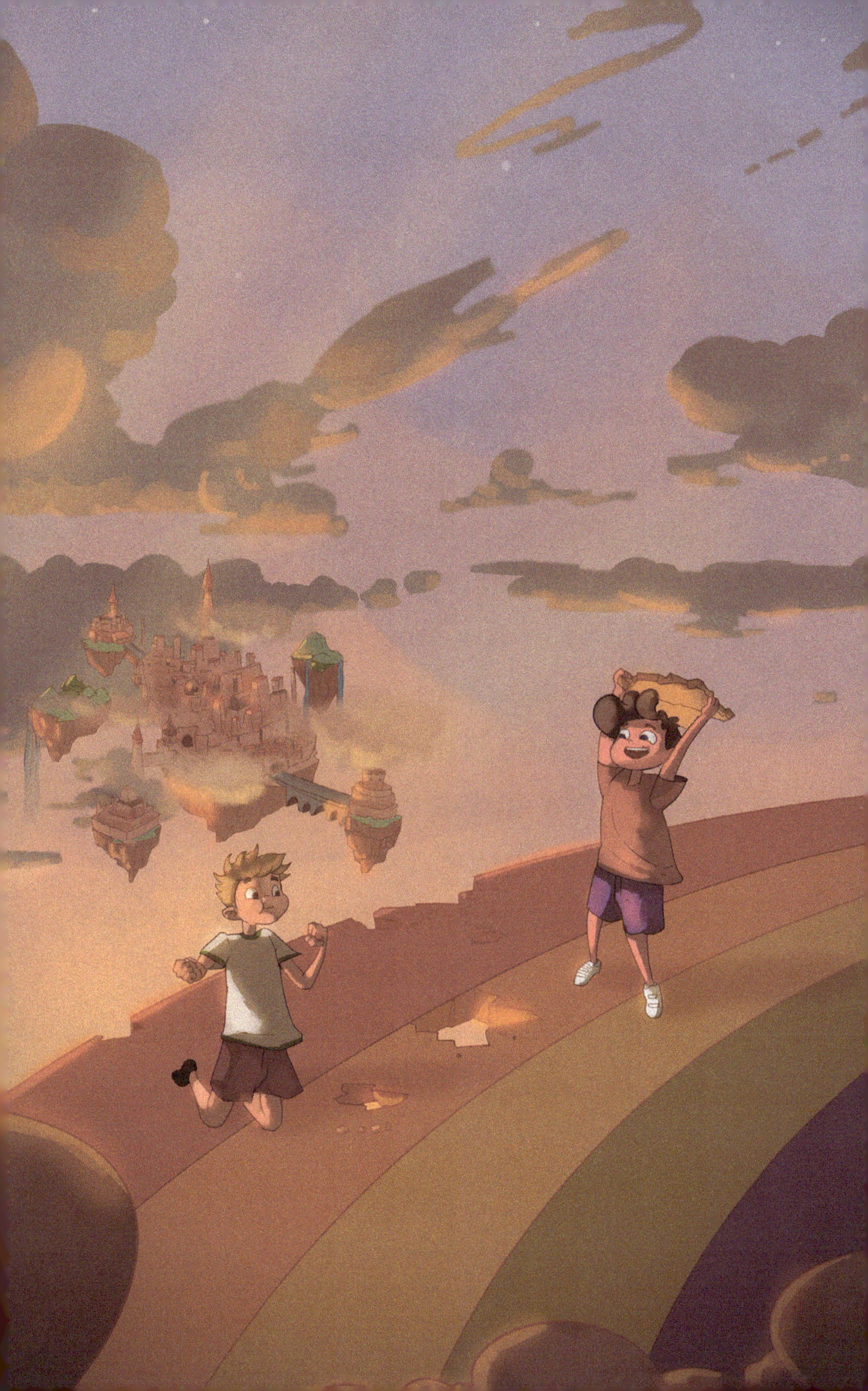

Marcus

I couldn't believe what stood before me. The great city of clouds 'Nubepollis'. I kept gaping at the colossal entity. The city shone golden in the sun; it was dawn.
It had towers and in between stuck a few houses. The architecture was modeled in such a way that they left plenty of open space.
Pappy was right, the nymphs do love the outdoors.
"Hey!" I heard a breathy voice call out for me. I turned to see a boy,

with a basket running towards me. He had baby blue skin and pointed ears.

"Were you born at night?" I ask him before anything else.

"That's a great way to introduce yourself, I'm Marcus," he replies with a smirk.

He was shorter than me and his pale blue skin glimmered in the morning sun.

"I'm sorry Marcus, I was startled and it was rude of me to ask that abruptly. I'm Joshua, just call me Josh. I'm only called Joshua when in trouble," I said.

Marcus chuckles, he finds it hilarious.

"Yes, I was born at night, you do know a few things about us cloud nymphs."
"Pappy, my grandpa told me all about you. I can't believe I'm here!" I start jumping with excitement.
"Josh, want a Chika?" He offered the famous Chika fruit as he had a load of them in his basket.
"My mom's making some Cuskis, it's a sweet delicacy made from Chikas,"
he explained.
Marcus cut the prickly top off with a small knife, apparently, everyone carried it around.

I bit into my Chika. The sweetness blew my mind. How could something this delicious even exist in this world, how unfair that nature's gift only existed in the clouds.

It was soft, blue flesh, and the sweet fragrance it gave away attracted me furthermore.

"It's your first time having a Chika I suppose?" he asked.

"Yes, we don't find it on earth," I answered while gobbling my fruit up.

"It's a staple food here but we keep hearing from foreigners like you that it's the best food you've ever tasted," he says.

I was a mess, blue essence all over my hands and mouth. He laughed uncontrollably, "Let's go to my house and you can wash up there."
He snapped his fingers and we were up in the air, a cloud lifted us, I gasped and shrieked.
"Calm down," he said.
We soared above the cloud city, which glistened like glitter in the sunlight. We then stooped low to narrow down into a beautiful neighborhood. We stopped in front of a white house. "Come on" Marcus motioned me to follow him. My eyes were feasting upon the beauty this house projected.

I touched the walls to find them smooth, I realized that they were clouds. "Marcus, how is it possible? Your home it's made up of clouds?" I was astonished.
He started chuckling, "You should know by now that there are different types of clouds and winds. The clouds we use to build our homes are different, they are hardened with water and are sturdy against some winds. We can carry our homes with us and change our location. So, many things you need to learn about Nubepollis. Don't worry you're new here"
"Yeah…" I said, smiling a bit embarrassed.
"Marcus," his mother called out for him.

"Where's the basket? Oh... Hello there, you're his friend?" she asked me. She has mustard yellow, born in the day. Her voice was sweet but stern at the same time. When she smiled, it felt real and warm.

"Yes Ma'am, I'm Josh," I said.

"Josh you must be feeling hungry, dinner will be set up soon," she said with a kind face.

It didn't strike me at first, but then I realized that it was morning.

"Ma'am, is it dinner or breakfast?" I asked politely.

She chuckled and reminded me that nymphs sleep in the day to work at night.

"Mama, can I show Josh around?" he pleaded.
"Sure, but be back by 7," she instructed.
He held my hand and dragged me back from the porch. We settled down on a fluffy cloud.
"Cross your fingers for a rainbow."
"Why?" I asked.
He smirked and said, "You'll see."
We soared above the city again, a few passersby flew alongside us.
He took me further away from the city, near the outskirts.
"It drizzled some time ago. Wait, I think I found one." We made our way to where he was pointing at.

It was a seven-colored rainbow, a huge one. Its colors were very vivid and a pleasant aroma grew stronger as we closed on it.

It was so mesmerizing. It filled my soul with joy.

"Does a rainbow actually have gold at the ends, or is it just another myth?" I asked curiously, knowing nothing is impossible in Nubepollis.

"No, where did you hear that from? Why would a rainbow have gold?!"
he started chortling.

"Marcus, we're gonna crash!!!!!" I screamed. He veered the cloud at the exact moment. Luckily, we didn't crash into the rainbow.

"Sorry, my bad, we could have gotten hurt. The rainbow is actually solid here." He stood on the cloud and reached out for the rainbow.

He broke a piece from the red layer and offered it to me. He took another one and stuffed it in his mouth.

I followed him.

My tastebuds were filled with the sweetness of candy. The flavor reminded me of red cherries. He broke some more pieces from different layers,
each a new flavor.
The rainbow looked hilarious, if anyone from a distance spotted it, they would find small holes in between, like how a rat bites through clothes.
I started laughing and kept sucking on my rainbow candy.
He brought out a small pouch and filled it.
"These are for my little sister; she loves the yellow ones," he said, smiling softly.

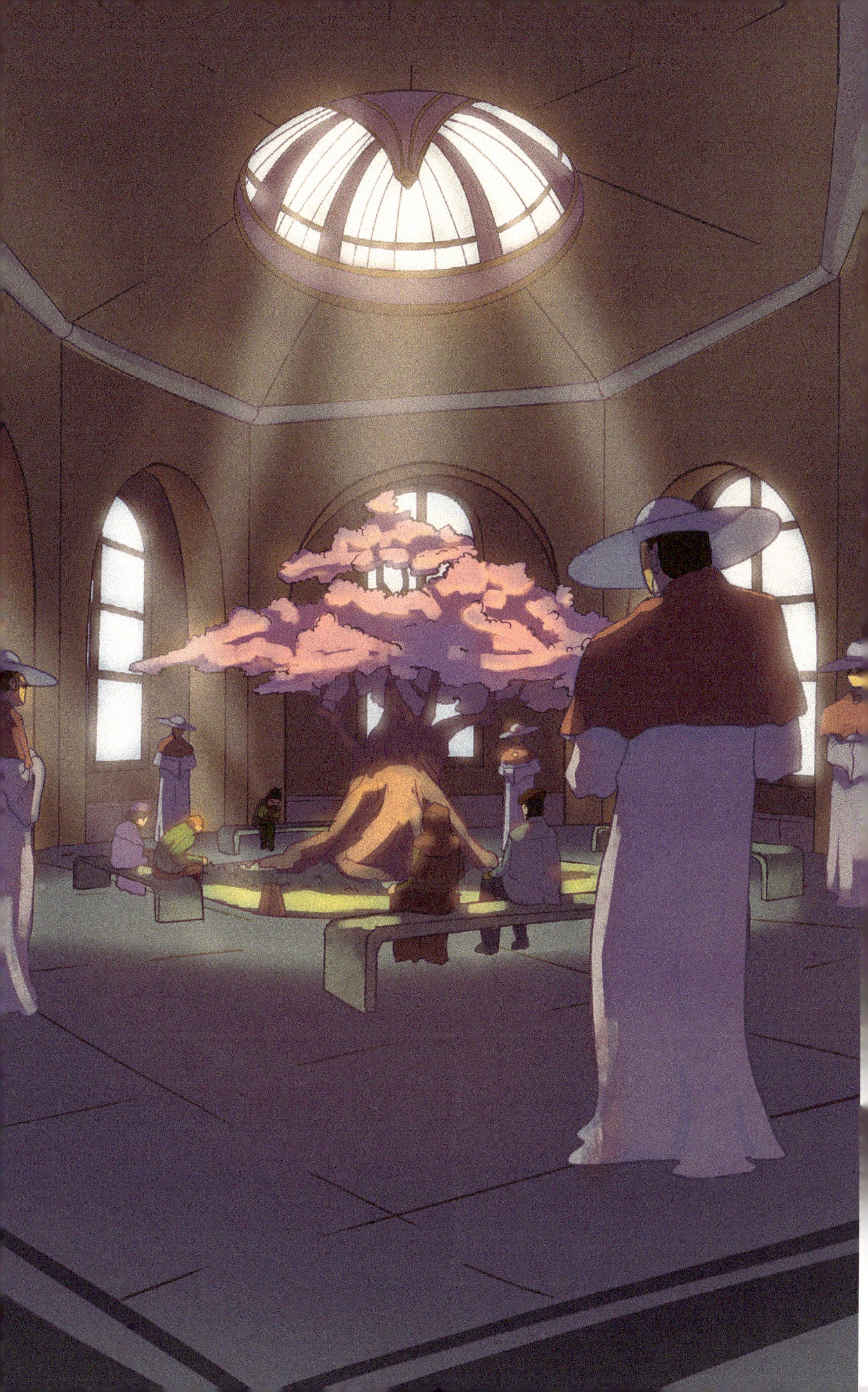

It must be nice to have a sibling; I wonder how it would have been if I were an elder brother.
They would all line up when I ask them to, I would be someone they would look up to. On the other hand, there would be a lot of responsibility.
I wonder if that role even befits me in the first place.
"Let's go home now, Mama is expecting us." He drove the cloud back home.
I introduced myself to Mr. Avel. He was an amiable man, who laughed at every silly joke or sentence.

Pappy says that when someone behaves like that it could only mean that they're trying to be very welcoming.

Pappy would always break the ice by cracking a joke or talking simply.

"Sir, how is it to work in the Theomagus?" I asked him.

The Theomagus is the place where the nymphs work.

"I bet you want me to describe the entire place?" His eyes sparkled. I simply nodded my head.

"In Theomagus, work and duty are allotted to different people belonging to different levels.

The highest level is reserved for the members of 'Elder Ones'. These higher ops are extremely powerful, wise, and talented. To qualify for this one must at least be 50 years old.
Next comes the 'Outreachers', which happens to be my level of the job. Many nymphs work as Outreaches.
We have another important level to monitor all these things, they're the 'Magistraus'.
Some nymphs ignore their duty and responsibility and fool around. The Magistraus catches them and puts them back to work. It would be a disaster every time a nymph missed their duty.

Nightmares would spread all around the globe," he ended with a gloomy note.

"Is it compulsory for all nymphs to work?" I questioned.

"No, not at all. We nymphs are actually quite proud of our responsibility. It's a hard thing to do. The shortlisting of names in service makes this job even more serious. Only the best of the best joins the Theomagus. But, as time passes by, some nymphs lose the determination and discipline they had in the beginning. This makes the Magistraus come into force.

There are other job opportunities too, passionate nymphs become architects, while others do arts and performances," he described.

We all cleared our dishes; the food was delicious. A delicacy to be frank. I wish Pappy learns how to cook better. Again, I can't blame him, since he started to learn the art of making food just a few years back.

It was bedtime for them, though the sun was high up in the sky. What surprised me the most was I too was feeling sleepy.

"Marcus, why do I feel sleepy?" I asked him.

"Josh, do you know another reason why we nymphs sleep in the morning?" he asked.

"No," I replied.
"Our magic gets drained in the sun. We gain our powers from the silver clouds and the celestial dust from heavenly stars. Our powers are the most sensitive in daylight, as the sun is too powerful for us.
The tender moonlight suits us the best to retain our magic." I understood every word.
Funny that I got reminded of vampires. But that didn't explain why I was feeling sleepy.
"Plus, the food we eat strengthens our magic, so you might feel sleepy since your body is adjusting to this," Marcus said.

"Wait, does that mean I have magic?" I asked, getting excited by the thought itself. I get excited way too easily.

"No silly, you just have magic but you can't wield it, after all you're not a nymph. Nymphs have some special features in their body which allow them to perform magic. We had this for a test in school, but I don't remember much exactly." And with that, all my hopes of being a human-nymph drowned.

When we woke up, the sun had already set, it was around 6:00 p.m. Marcus' little sister was still asleep so we took our time doing various chores. They didn't expect me to take part since I'm a visitor, but it was the least I could do for the dinner and their affability.
Mr. Avel left for work and we joined him too. I was all giddy since he was going to show me the Theomagus.

Theomagus

Our cloud landed in front of the sector. Theomagus is located in the heart of the great city, Nubepollis, where everyone seemed welcoming. The entire atmosphere was light and carefree. They were settling up for work, Mr. Avel described his job as an Outreach. Theomagus was alive, the shuffling of feet against the hard floor could be heard throughout the entire complex. They had a huge wall clock ticking, it only made everyone anxious. The wall clock had a huge dial and you could read the numbers from any corner!

The Magistraus were on patrol and checking on everyone. For nymphs, they were quite intimidating. They didn't interrogate me as Mr. Avel had my back and took complete responsibility for me. He is a kind man.

The Magistraus wore black robes with yellow stripes, unlike the others who wore casual clothing.

Their pointed ears, piercing looks, sharp eyes, and well-built frames heightened one's senses.

Some Outreachers who were unattentive previously were now perpetuated and uneasy.

It was 10:30 p.m. and all preparations were ready for the ritual.
We all shifted to the great hall. It was big enough to fit in half of the nymph population.
Mr. Avel led me and Marcus to the very front row. Everyone seated themselves on clouds that were half afloat from the ground.
The great hall held some of the most sacred elements in Nubepollis.
The biggest one so far was the 'Selenanthia' or the MoonFlower tree. This is the most sacred tree, and very rare to find.

"Josh, do you know why the MoonFlower is sacred?" Marcus asked me.
I didn't have an answer, of course, I didn't know!
"Well, what do we do when there is a new moon? How can we harvest power from celestial dust?
How can we provide dreams? If we don't then nightmares would plague the world.
The MoonFlower is a gift, brought into creation by the almighty for the sole purpose of harvesting celestial dust. When there is no moon, we use the MoonFlower's magic light."

I looked up at the tree again. It was like an oak tree, but its branches spread out more and the leaves were between yellow and green.

There were no flowers, only buds that sprouted at every turn. "Marcus, what about the flowers?"

"The flowers bloom during every new moon, the great tree stores energy from the moonlight whenever possible. It makes the best of the moonlight," he explained.

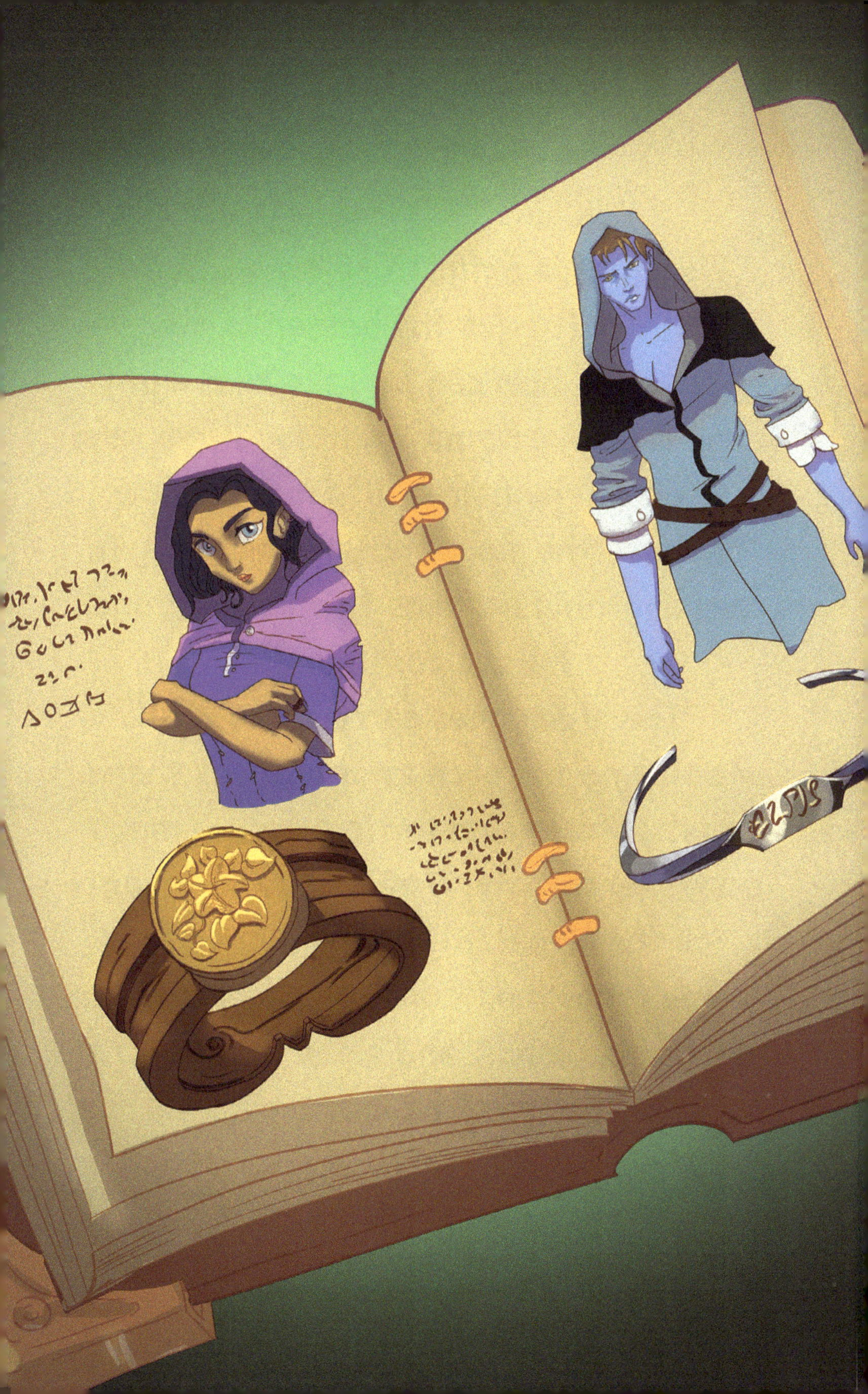

"Is this the only MoonFlower alive?" Curiosity got the better of me.

"No silly, how can we take such a big risk! We have MoonFlower seedlings, and some of them are quite mature now. We have the next MoonFlower ready in case anything happens to the great one," Marcus continued.

"The elder ones carry some vital tools and the enchanter creates these tools. The enchanter is a very famous craftsperson, she creates the best tools for the ritual. All of her ingredients come from the MoonFlower, gems from the hidden lands, and some other secret recipes," he narrated.

"You seem to know her?" I raised my eyebrows, asking him.
"Yes, for she's my aunt," he said plainly.
"Your Aunt?! I didn't know that," I exclaimed.
"You don't know many things, Josh," he said with a grin.
I rolled my eyes and continued the conversation.
"She's seated right over there..." Marcus pointed at his aunt. She was chatting with another nymph; they were a few seats away from us.
"Aunt Liliac!" he called out her name.

She glanced in our direction and excused herself.
She smiled as she made her way towards us.
"If it isn't my favorite nephew," she said, patting his back.
"Liliac, you said that to my sister the last time," he replied. She gave an embarrassed smile and continued.
"What are you doing here?" she asked him without noticing my presence.
"I'm here with Josh, Papa brought us here for the ritual." He pointed at him.
"Oh, sorry Josh, I didn't see you there," she apologized sweetly.

I'm not invisible to be ignored like that, I thought.

"So, Josh, what brings you to Nubepollis? Young boys like you don't come up here much," she commented.

"I'm here to learn more about this great city, it fascinates me a lot... You see Ma'am, my grandpa, Pappy told me all he knew about Nubepollis and its lovely citizens.

We come from a family of explorers, I am just living up to my family tradition, I love having an adventure on a side note," I explained.

She grinned "Ah... That's a nice cause Josh. I have to sa..." She was cut in between with an alarming sound.
"Boys, talk to you later, break's over now." And with that, she left us to ourselves.
Before I could ask Marcus, what was happening, the chief Magistraus banged his staff to the ground and barked a command "Salute!" Everyone stood up, rigid and attentive.
Footsteps clanged against the floor as these nymphs traveled to the center of the great hall.

They wore crimson red robes on top of their attire.

Everyone took their seats once the red-robed nymphs settled down.

"They're the great Elder Ones," Marcus whispered in my ear.

Their faces were visible clearly as we were seated right in the front. They lacked any signs of aging, in fact, they looked younger than most nymphs here. Their faces were clear of any wrinkles, tight skin, and a lack of any white hair.

"Why do they look young?" I muttered.

"Long story short, they are the highest order with great powers in magic. So, they naturally look like that,"
he Responded.
I tried to make sense of the ritual as much as I could.
Marcus lent me his childhood handbook on nymph magic which explained some major aspects of the ritual.
The five Elder Ones each brought out their magic tools or possessions. These tools were carved from the MoonFlower tree. Every Elder One wielded a unique possession.
One had a ring made with wood from MoonFlower and its bud always growing and on it. Every New Moon the bud

blossoms into a full-grown MoonFlower and helps with the ritual. This special ring is called 'Selena' named after its famous user.

The second possession belonged to Annas, handed down from his mother, a priestess. This is a bracelet made of silver, it is the most sacred metal to the Nymphs. It helps sustain magic longer equally when compared to the MoonFlower.

Generally, silver isn't advised since it is hard to control. The wielder must have certain strong characteristics which many nymphs lack. This is why nymphs rarely use silver.

Annas' bracelet has the word 'Elpis' engraved into it.
Elpis is a spirit of hope, the very message the nymphs spread.
The third Elder One is rather quite young. He became a member at thirty-one, which in human age is equivalent to just twenty. Thaddeus was an exceptional case, his power, control, and coordination were on par with the Elder Ones. He was a sensation in the cloud world. The Elder Ones are very selective, hard for any higher up to qualify for the big position. They chose him not for his powers, but for his ability to lead and judge. He is a righteous nymph, who is sincere and idealistic in all terms.

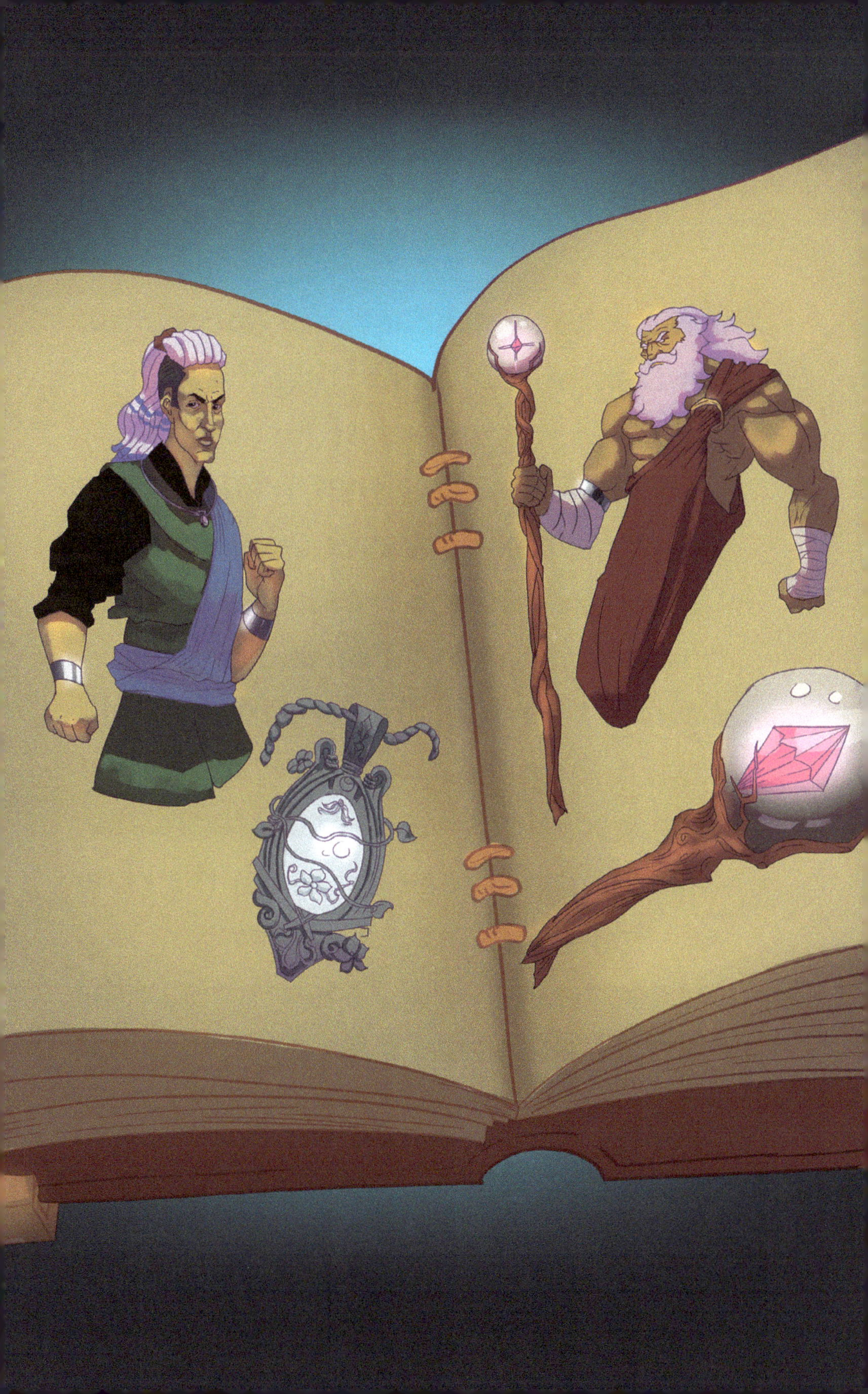

Thaddeus has a pendant, the MoonFlower wood entwined, connecting the pearl, born in the waters of Innocence. Innocence is a river that trails down the wonderland forests, where many mythical beasts and treasures lie. Only those with great valor and courage are able to attain this precious pearl, found in the mouth of the river. Quite a few generations have encountered the chance to own this pearl, which the river Innocence produces rarely.

The fourth Elder One, Prometheus is the oldest of all, he has been a member for the past two generations. His face shows signs of aging, some wrinkled skin, and tired eyes, but not much again since they're nymphs.

He is known for his tactfulness and the vast knowledge he holds. He devises most of the planning and is generally known as the brains behind the Elder Ones.

He is humble and there's always a lot to learn from him. His methods aren't conventional, for he is a broad thinker.

He wields a long staff made from MoonFlower wood, the silver ball on the top, protects the magenta-colored gem which is the core.

The fifth and final Elder One, Talia. She's the chief, the head, and the most well-known Elder One. She has taken tough decisions during hard times and many commend her for that. She has gained public trust and became the face of the Elder Ones. She is an iron-willed nymph and her sense of judgment is incomparable. She is virtuous and follows her core principles that led her to such heights.

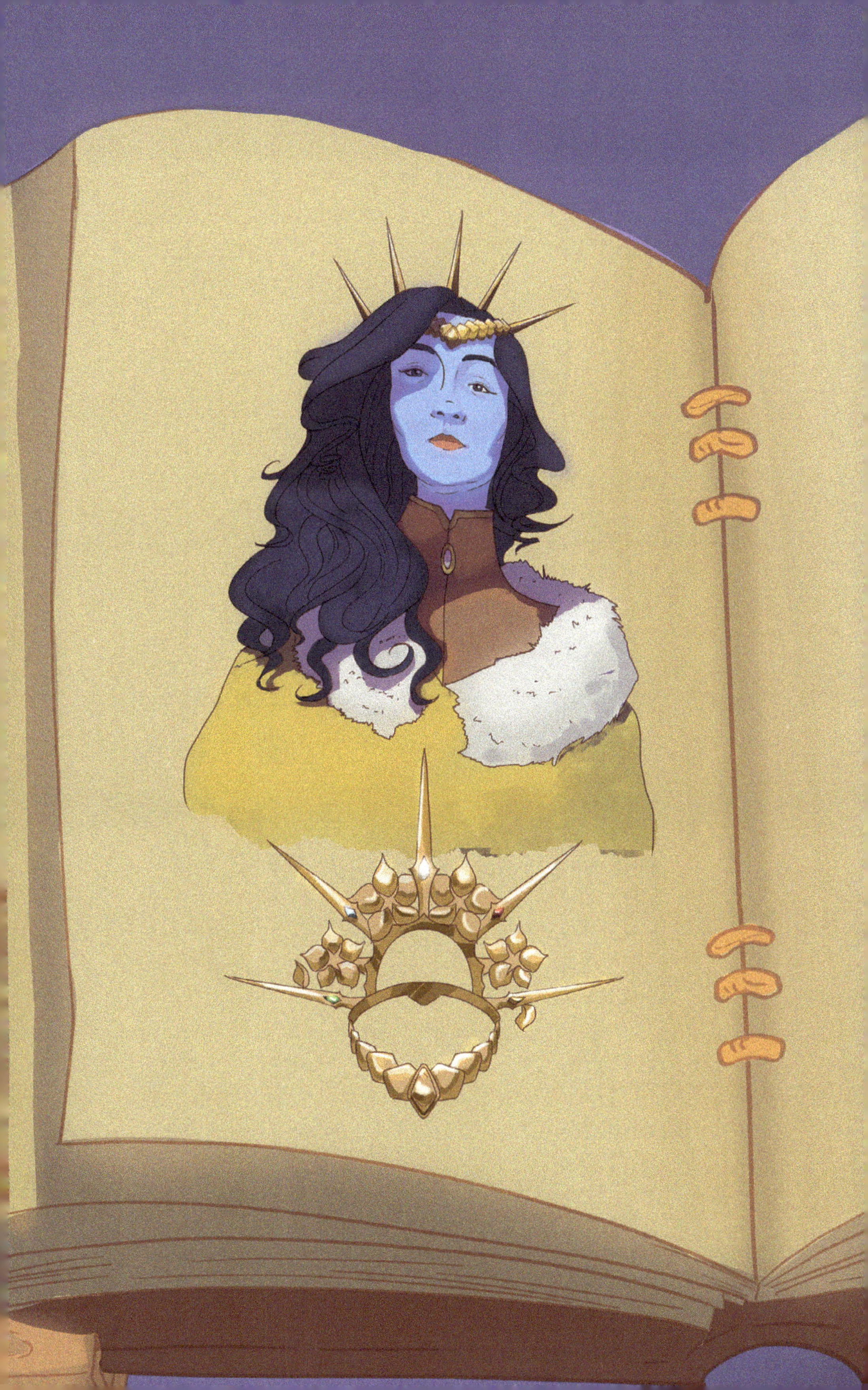

Talia's crown is the most powerful one, it has versatile properties which makes it achieve this power. The crown is made from MoonFlower branches, with silver curves, dented with the all-knowing crystals.
Each crystal representing each element: Jade for the earth, Aquamarine for water, White Quartz for wind, Garnet for fire, and Citrine for light.
This was all about the Elder Ones, I bet there are a lot more unrecorded facts about them.

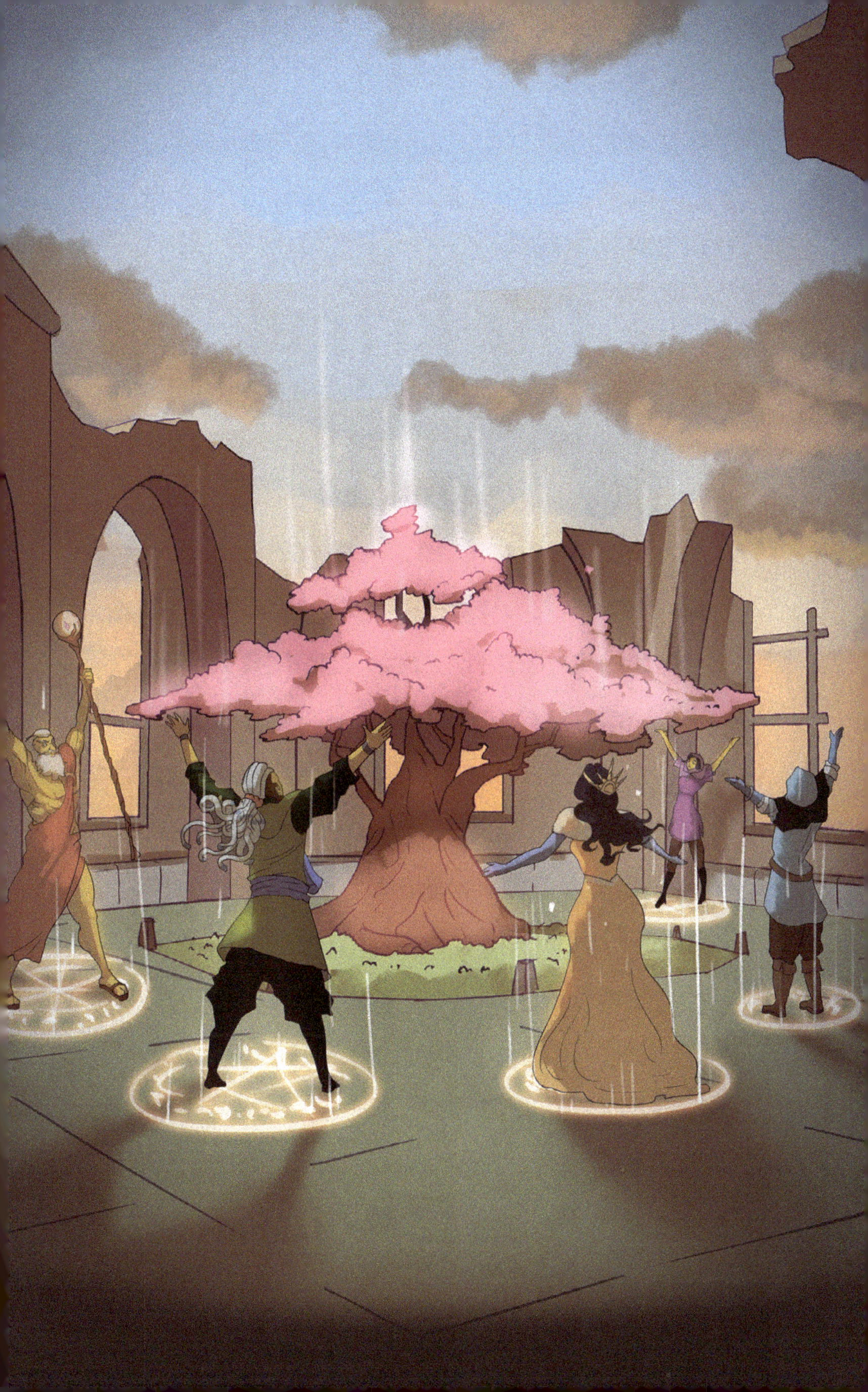

The Ritual

The great five Elder Ones began the ritual. They brought out their magical possessions.

The floor they stood on had various designs and patterns carved into it. Each spot they stood in had curved lines, spirals on top of each other, flowers, and other ingenious forms. They reminded me of Persian rugs and floor mat designing found in Indian homes, but were even more complicated and on an entirely another level.

The Elder Ones performed a dance, they hopped to each spiral design, which glowed blue. They took their positions now, with some spirals activated while others looked plain. They tapped their feet with such synchronization that it surprised me. The blue glow turned violently into a sizzling bright flame. My eyes were trapped and swooned by the dancing flames.

They weren't even bothered by the flame; they closed their eyes for a moment. Their magical tools were held up high, pointed upwards, and were inclined to connect.

The air got colder and felt damp, each Elder One's tool gave out a different color, lighting up the room with blazing lights.
The ring gave a purple hue, the bracelet a red, the staff a green color, the pendant a yellow and the crown gave off white.
The clouds which formed the roof parted away allowing the bright moon to shine upon us. These wonderful lights lit up the pitch-black sky in addition to the moonlight.
The MoonFlower hummed and indigo fireflies buzzed all around it, that's

what I thought and mistook it for till Marcus corrected me later.

The buzzing fireflies are the essence of the MoonFlower tree, which is scattered from the sky, to fall and implant in people's dreams. These fireflies are called 'Phren'. These are secondary measures for creating dreams.

As the colors spread through the sky, it reminded me of northern lights. I turned to ask Marcus a question and was shocked to find some weird markings on his face. I nearly screamed, and that's when he

placed his hand on my mouth.
"Look at yourself." He pointed out.
I gasped as I stared at my hands.
"Goodness heavens…" I remarked.
There were some unknown patterns formed on my skin. It was ink-black in color, I didn't even feel anything when this happened, it was out of the blue.
"Psst…" Marcus signaled for me, he shoved the book into my arms and pointed at the index page.
I didn't read everything, so I happened to be unprepared for this. I gave him a cheeky smile, and it ticked me off when he rolled his eyes.
Ugh! I cursed internally.

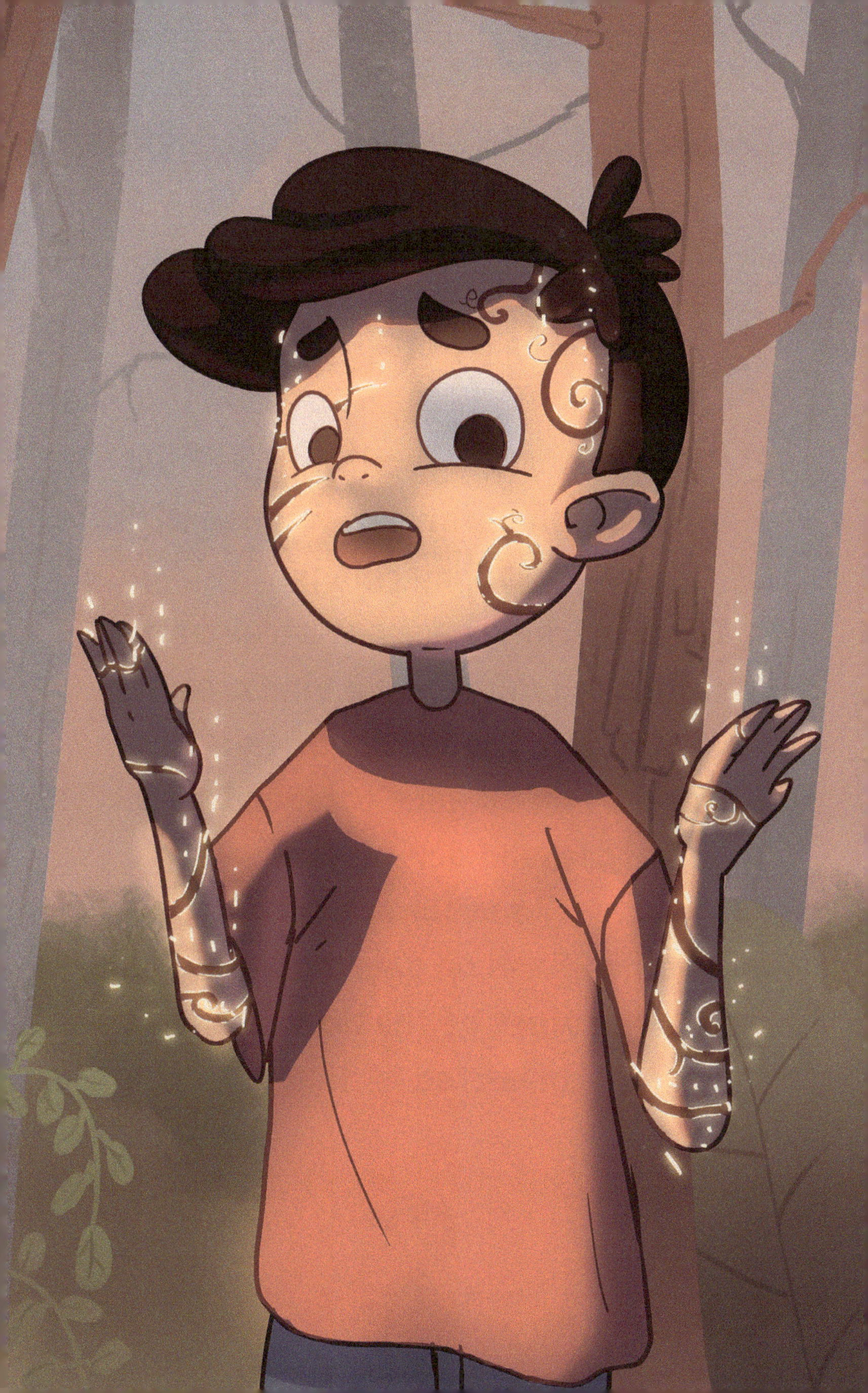

I flipped to page 38 and read the contents in my mind.
It said:
'All those taking part in the ritual will find themselves tattooed with black markings.
These markings are not straight but rather are more like a vine crawling your skin. The leaves of this vine are drawn on your ears, and your forehead depicts a single MoonFlower bud.
The vines form on your body to signal that the vines of the MoonFlower are connected with you.

Fun Fact: This bud blooms into a complete flower once you enter the 'Parodos'.
*We'll explain this on the next page.'
I gave a glance to every single Nymph I could spot and they all had this. Someone stamped on my foot, I winced with pain and saw Marcus motioning me to continue reading.
It must have been important.
'Now, you youngsters must be feeling the urge to get some tattoos on yourself, probably using a marker could get you one, but your parents would be annoyed with it.

Next comes the most important feat of the ritual, drumroll, please. PARODOS!!!
So, what about Parodos, is it even important in the first place?
To answer all your questions, yes, it is very important. It's like a terminal which you enter to or exit from.
You will enter the Oneiroi through the portal created, and this portal is called Parodos.
Oneiroi is where all the dreams happen. Your consciousness will roam in the lands of Oneiroi, your body will stay intact in the ritual room.' I read.
I was wondering if I had reached the Parodos, so I pinched his hand to grab

his attention. He mouthed ouch and glared at me. Payback that's what I thought.

I pointed at my forehead and questioned him, he signed 10, which assumed were minutes.

I could see the flower almost blooming on his forehead.

It must have been 10 seconds, so anytime now, I thought.

I felt drowsy, the urge to sleep was beyond tempting and I couldn't fight. My eyes were heavier than a sack of wet cotton, forcing me into a deep slumber.

I felt bliss until I got whacked in the head with something menacing.

I jerked awake only to be consumed by vast spaces of whiteness.

"Hey!" I heard Marcus' voice nearby.

"Josh, are you alright?" he asked me, lending me a hand to get me on my feet.

"Yes. I think someone hit my head with a log or a rod," I complained.

"Ah... I know how you're feeling, it was even worse for me the first time I got here," he said sourly.

"Where am I again?" I asked uncertainly, staring at the empty blankness.

"Welcome to Oneiroi, the land of dreams and sleep," he announced proudly.

"This is such a disappointment!" I blurted out.

"Huh? What do you mean?" he demanded.

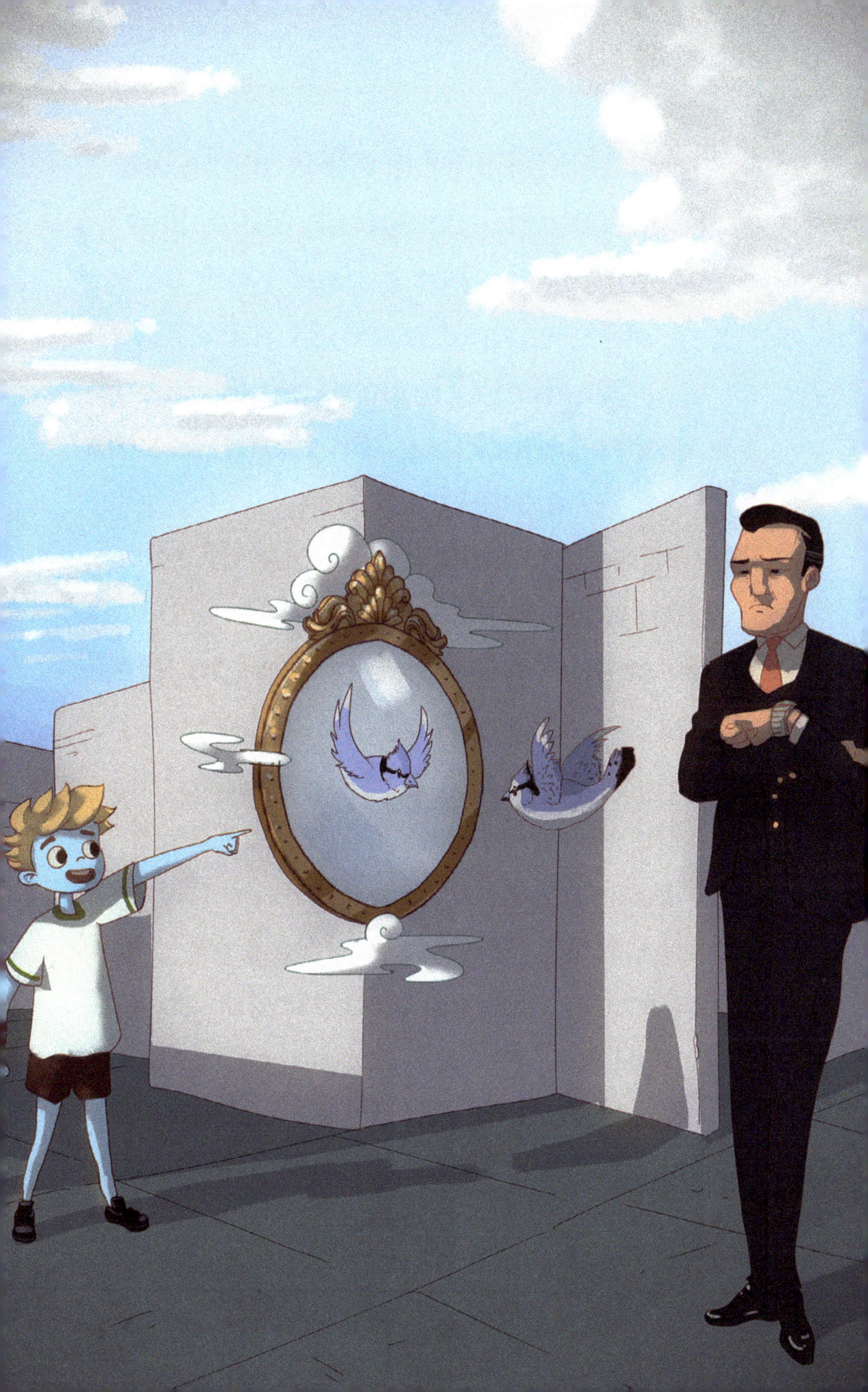

"Isn't the land of dreams supposed to be colorful, magical, alive, and everything in that sense? I can only see whitewashed walls, is this truly Oneiroi?" I questioned.

He started chuckling "Oh that... Let me explain to Josh."

"Imagine this vast multitude of empty whitespace as a canvas, where you can draw anything and bring them to life."

I was starting to understand where he was leading this to.

"Ah, there you are boys. I've been searching for you all over the place. Now, Now stay around me, the Magistraus are very particular about discipline." Mr. Avel fumbled around and brought out a waist clock.

"Father, could you please show him the magic of Oneiroi?" Marcus pleaded.

"Ah, of course, it's not a big deal. Just observe me doing my job. You can see other nymphs like me, we're the 'Outreachers'. We conjure the dreams of sleeping minds." With that, Mr. Avel snapped his fingers.

I was up in the air, at least 20 feet above the so-called ground. "Whoa!" I exclaimed.

"Not to worry, we're all working in Oneiroi. It's only our consciousness here. Our mortal bodies back at Theomagus," Mr. Avel reassured me. "Josh, you can do anything here. Just think of it from the deepest parts of your heart and it will happen." Marcus demonstrated, by soaring around in the air with his wings that appeared out of thin air.

I too wanted to fly. Oh, the free and open sky was always delightful. The birds truly know what it means to be alive, they fly every day, going around in loops and groups, and live for the very air.

My heart raced, I could feel my pulse beating faster and my ears popping. Argh! AAAA... I screamed frantically, but all that came out were squawks like a bird.

"My oh my! Josh, you're a bird. No, it's more of, 'You're a Blue Jay!'"
he exclaimed.
I was flapping my feathers hard, I managed to transform into a bird.
"See for yourself." he said and conjured a mirror.
I saw my light blue feathers, smooth and well preened. My feathers were beautifully patterned, and my black beak looked sharp. I was a Blue Jay.
'Nothing can stop me now, I'm invincible!' I smirked internally.
I was flowing with new profound powers, I felt magical.

My thoughts of ruling the world were interrupted by Mr. Avel, "Boys, I'm afraid we would have to stop our share of fun now," he said warily.

From above, I could see a vast maze of white walls under us. Some Outreachers were already on their job and this maze spread out till infinity. The Magistraus eyed us with a look of annoyance on their faces.

"Let's transform and land, I have a lot more to show and explain," Mr. Avel insisted.

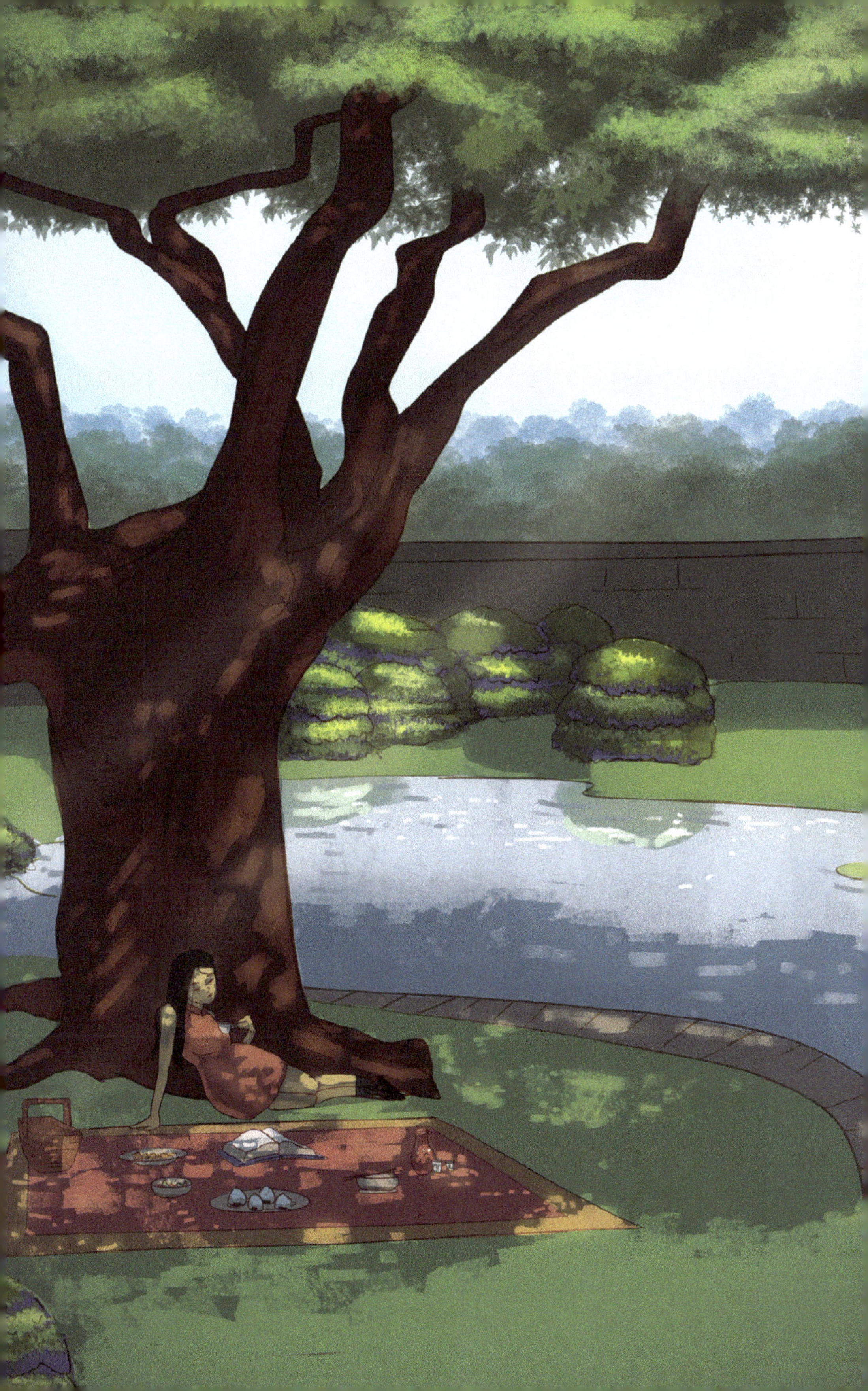

Oneiroi

We stooped low to the ground and stopped in front of a white wall. "This is called 'Psyche'." Mr. Avel stated.
The so-called 'Psyche' or in my language 'White-wall' seemed to give away some radiance.
I looked puzzled, "Place your hand on it." Mr. Avel demonstrated.
As soon as I touched the tepid wall, I could hear voices that then toned down. I was able to see a human. Her face seemed a bit blur, but I was able to understand her, she didn't need to say anything. Things seemed calm and that's when these voices erupted into a fury.

The world started spinning around, my head was on fire.

These voices murmured, hissed, and spat the ugliest words out of their wretched mouths. They were troubling me, I felt tears running down my cheek. "STOP... Please, I beg you, stop," I whimpered.

That's when I snapped out of it. I was a mess, and wheezing hard. "She is troubled and in pain. These voices they're torturing her. Nishiyama is her name. She's a victim to these voices too. These voices are called Epiales. They originate from your mind's deepest fears. They cause nightmares sometimes," Mr. Avel explained with a gloomy look.

The nymphs who serve for this cause, they're great beings. Saving someone from collapsing into their own fears, they witness the worst too. They're heroes in my eyes, even better than Superman and Spiderman.

I've never felt this much gratitude before, I whispered "Mr. Avel, thank you for keeping us safe."

He grinned and replied, "It's our duty, Josh, it's our job. You don't have to thank us for that." I nodded my head.

"Let me ease her pain," he uttered and pressed his thumb and index fingers together. They glowed blue and the Psyche hummed.

"It's radiating a different color!" I pointed out.

"A yellow radiance means we have to work on it, a blue would say it's safe now, if we spot a red, we stay out of its way, and green would hint that we don't have to touch it," he explained.

"Father, what dream are you showing her?" Marcus asked inquisitively.

Mr. Avel snapped his fingers. The Psyche flickered and a picture came into view.

There was a scenic garden, with Cherry Blossom trees filling the space. A red striped mat laid down on the grass seemed inviting with crackers, rice balls, and other Japanese snacks. Nishiyama sat on one side, sipping hot tea and inhaling the marvelous beauty in front of her.
I read manga and comic books in my free time, and I have a few Japanese friends, they show me their pictures with Cherry Blossoms in the background.

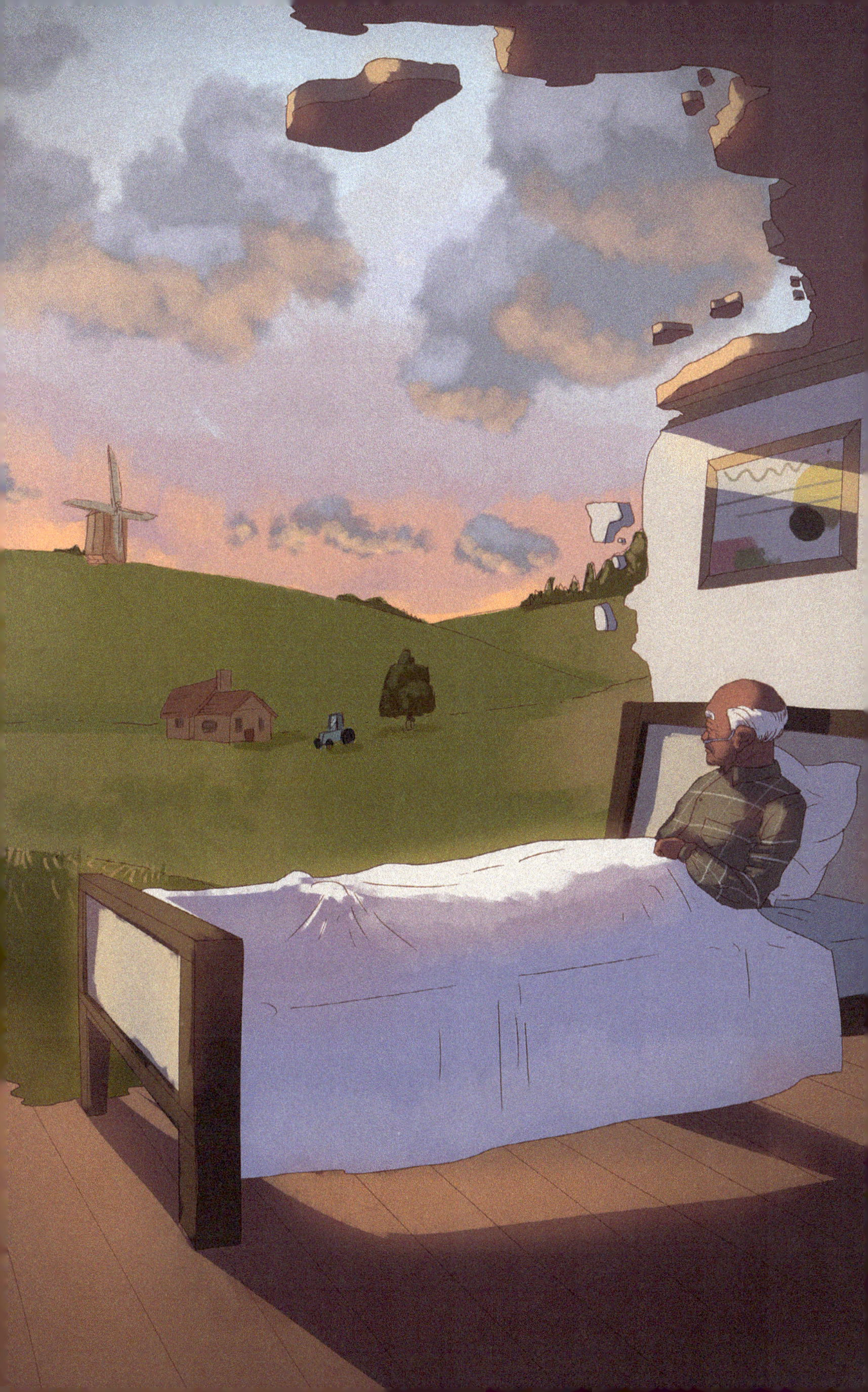

I felt happy for her. "Shall we move ahead with the tour now?" Mr. Avel teased.

"Yes sir!" I saluted him. I do this plenty of times, just to show that I'm serious.

"Hey, Marcus?"

"Yes?"

"How many times have you been here, in Oneiroi?" I interrogated him.

His face drooped, "You're assuming at least a few times if I'm not wrong." I nodded in agreement.

"I've been here only once before you. This is frankly my second time," he said with utter disappointment.

"No worries, Josh, you see I'll be working in Theomagus too!" he declared.

"Weren't you planning on taking architecture?" I reminded him, casually licking my choco-chip flavored ice cream I conjured out of nowhere.

He glared into my soul, "What? You want one?" I innocently asked offering another ice cream.

"No." He grunted and stomped his feet. I smirked, knowing I'd got on his nerves. We passed by different Psyches belonging to different people.

"There are so many here... Mr. Avel, how do you manage to sort them out?"

I questioned.

"This section of Oneiroi is reserved only for a special class of Outreachers. There are different tiers and levels, based on your experience or capabilities. We're on the professional side, this is where Marcus hasn't been before, that's why he's staring wide-eyed at everything." He winked.

"For the beginners, since they're new to this or just interns, they handle the sorted sections, so they don't have to worry about messing up. The intermediates handle the mid-sections, where things aren't relatively hard unlike the wild," he narrated.

"Hold up, we're on the wild side of Oneiroi?" I gasped.

"Nothing to worry about... Oh, a green psyche!" the man galloped his way there.

We placed our palms on the psyche, I felt nothing.

I raised my eyebrows in suspicion.

"You can't feel or hear or even see anything Josh," Marcus answered.

"This psyche is in deep sleep, in the beyond. Sometimes you don't dream of anything when you sleep, this is exactly what this Psyche's doing," he continued.

It made sense to me. Mr. Avel clapped his hands once and all the blue radiating Psyches piled up.

Images and visions moved in each Psyche. Two kids were playing in the playground, a man got his first bike and was flying over the hills in Sicily, a young teen dreamed of being the first female president of the United States, one became rich and was swimming in pools of gold, there all types of dreams, from the silliest to the most emotional. The only thing that mattered was that these people were safe, happy, in their pleasant dreams. Their psyche reflected warmth and tenderness.

"There have been some popular dreams, like these." He showed me.

"Ethan!" I gasped in surprise.
"Your friend I presume," Marcus guessed.
Ethan fell sick with the flu from what I recall, he appears to be even more active in his dreams than usual. Mr. Avel played his dream.
His black hair was styled differently from his usual trim. He seemed to have applied gel and was dressed in a fancy suit.
"Sir, she's here," announced an old male voice from the corner.
"Alfred, get my 'Batmobile' ready, eh," he ordered.

The scene shifted to a lovely woman, whom I immediately recognized.
"My lady, you look gorgeous. That red dress fits you perfectly." He kissed her hand like a gentleman and led her into the Batmobile.
"You have pretty eyes," Diana Prince commented.
Ethan was blushing like a vermillion. Ethan is half Chinese, he always felt insecure about his eyes, we've always comforted him. He has to accept himself because we are born to stand out, not to fit in.
"Uh... Alfred, you can take a day off today," he suggested.

"Oh! my kind master. Have a great time sir," Alfred gushed over him.

In between, they saved the city from some villains. There was a point where Ethan got outnumbered by the gangsters. Diana Prince came to the rescue and kicked their butts.

He stood on the Batmobile to just give a hug, he's a kid who hasn't hit puberty yet. I too didn't for that matter.

"Mr. Avel, can we please continue with the tour, Ethan is gonna face hell once I return home," I growled with a scowl.

"Josh, you don't have to tell him about Nubepollis. It's better for them like this," he warned.

I nodded my head in agreement.
"Father," Marcus began.
"Yes?" answered Mr. Avel, and that's when we heard two voices.
We both shrieked in shock, witnessing two Mr. Avels.
"Papa, you scared me." Marcus let out a sigh.
Both the clones were roaring with laughter.
"It's not funny!" exclaimed Marcus.
"I'm sorry, but both of your expressions were priceless," he apologized, wiping a tear out of his eye.

"I always work like this, I split myself up into many clones to increase the efficiency of work," he explained.
"So, they're not your mirror images?" I asked cautiously.
"No." Both of them disagreed.
"Father, that Psyche needs help. We better rush." Marcus ended the conversation.
The psyche was radiating yellow light. Mr. Avel did a few gestures with his fingers. It turned blue, and the white wall started playing the dream.
An old man was coughing hard with fever and chills.

Sweat beaded on his dark skin. He was trembling with fear and sickness. "Darla, my love. I'll meet ya soon." "Honey, they haven't arrived yet. I'm doing my best to sustain the burning flame, just a bit longer. Our lovely daughters and sons. I asked Darius to send them all letters about my present state. Agh... They replied, saying they were busy and would come by this weekend. Darling, I wish you stood by my deathbed first instead of making me do that for you." His hoarse voice struggled. He wept and sobbed, his lonely heart ached for warmth and love.

"Darla, we did a lot for them. We protected them when there was no protection for us people of color. We did a great job together honey. They've turned out into wonderful beings. I'm glad I get to leave seeing them safe and sound. Oh… Darla." He took his last breath and the room grew silent.

Mr. Avel snapped his fingers. The dream shifted to another. The old man now looked young and strong. His family was having a great time at his mother's house.

He kissed his wife with joy, and four of his kids were frolicking around on the farm. He felt content and happy.
The sun was setting upon them, a new beginning for them.
"Kids, time for supper," Darla called out. "I love you, honey." He embraced her into a hug.
The dream faded away. "Mr. Avel, I'm glad he's better now." I cried. The atmosphere felt sad and dreary now. We kept walking forward and encountered many psyches. Time flew by and I never noticed.
"Josh, there isn't much time left

for your departure. I'm afraid you would have to leave Nubepollis now," Mr. Avel explained.

"I should leave now?!" I gave him puppy eyes.

"That wouldn't affect me," he replied bluntly.

"But, Father, why can't he stay longer," Marcus questioned.

"Josh, you have to return to the ground. You have another day to start, and the night has already passed." I sighed.

"On the bright note, you can visit us anytime you want to. Just remember that before sleeping, think about us, think about Nubepollis and this magical world. We'll find you for sure," he ended.

I didn't have to worry much if that's the case.

I gave Marcus a hug and a high fi, thanked Mr. Avel for his hospitality (Pappy insists I be polite).

"See ya tomorrow!" I exclaimed. "You're leaving Oneiroi and Nubepollis in two seconds." And with that, I left the magical land of dreams.

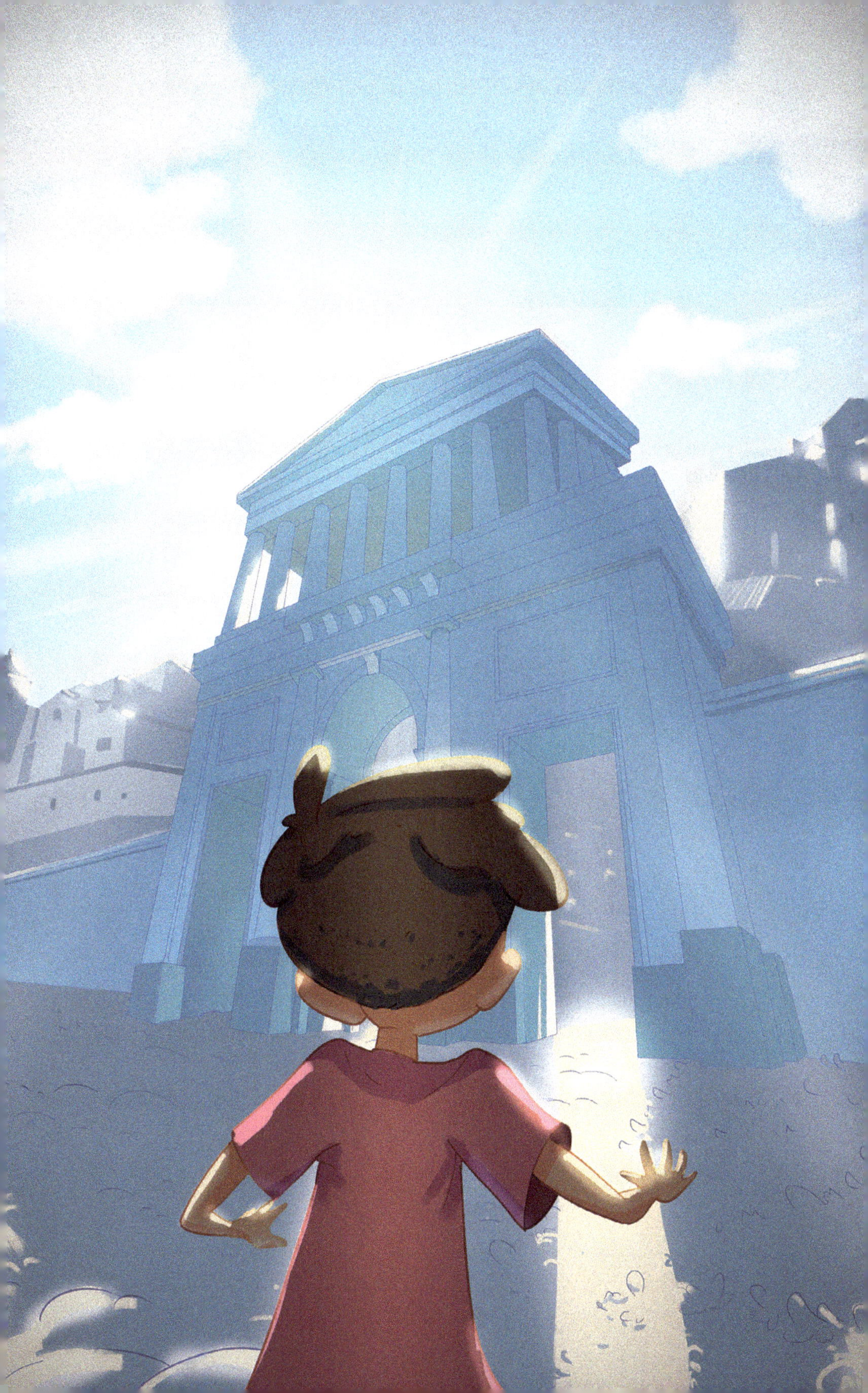

Another Day

I rubbed my eyes and gave a loud yawn.
"You're up junior." Pappy smiled.
I realized I was in my bedroom. "Did we go camping yesterday, Pappy?!"
"Yes, why? Don't you remember?"
I grinned in relief, "Nah, I just got confused."
"I'm sorry junior, you must have hit your head hard."
"Hit my head?" I raised my eyebrows to question him.
"Yes, while entering the room your head bumped a bit into the door. You were sleeping like a baby, I had to

carry you out of the car, you know," he complained.

"It's not like you had to carry me all the way from the creek," I mumbled.

"Joshua..." He put on his malicious expression.

"Pappy, I've been to Nubepollis, and you won't believe me. Me and my friend Mar..." He cut me swiftly by saying, "Yes, I know Marcus and Mr. Avel. You kept muttering their names over and over. I got creeped out a bit. Giving your old man a fright." He took me by surprise.

"Tell me what happened while having breakfast, I prepared some waffles,

so come down quick." With that he left.
"Oh boy, could my day get any better."
Sunshine peeked through my curtain,
just how every season passes through
my life. I will become a renowned and
talented explorer, discovering new
magical worlds.

Dreams that cave a path for my journey
with only pit stops and no destination
in sight. A wonderful life it is.

CPSIA information can be obtained
at www.ICGtesting.com
Printed in the USA
BVHW091425240223
659163BV00011B/513